Emma & Greasy

the Biggest Little Farm
Saving Emma the Pig

by **JOHN CHESTER**

illustrated by **JENNIFER L. MEYER**

FEIWEL & FRIENDS
NEW YORK

APRICOT LANE
— Farms —
EST 2011

Apricot Lane Farms is located in Moorpark, California. Our mission is to create a well-balanced ecosystem and rich soils that produce nutrient-dense foods while treating the environment and the animals with respect.

Our farm residents include pigs, goats, sheep, chickens, ducks, guinea hens, horses, highland cattle, and one brown Swiss dairy cow named Maggie. Our land consists of biodynamic certified avocado and lemon orchards, a vegetable garden, pastures, and over seventy-five varieties of stone fruit.

A Feiwel and Friends Book

An imprint of Macmillan Publishing Group, LLC

175 Fifth Avenue, New York, NY 10010

SAVING EMMA THE PIG: THE BIGGEST LITTLE FARM

Text copyright © 2019 by John Chester.

Illustrations copyright © 2019 by Jennifer L. Meyer.

All rights reserved. Printed in China by RR Donnelley Asia Printing Solutions Ltd., Dongguan City, Guangdong Province.

Our books may be purchased in bulk for promotional, educational, or business use.

Please contact your local bookseller or the Macmillan Corporate and Premium Sales Department at

(800) 221-7945 ext. 5442 or by email at MacmillanSpecialMarkets@macmillan.com.

Library of Congress Cataloging-in-Publication Data

Names: Chester, John (John G.) author. | Meyer, Jennifer L., illustrator.

Title: Saving Emma the pig / John Chester ; illustrated by Jennifer Meyer.

Description: First edition. | New York : Feiwel and Friends, 2019.

Identifiers: LCCN 2018039239 | ISBN 9781250187796 (hardcover)

Subjects: LCSH: Swine—California—Juvenile literature. | Farm

life—California—Anecdotes—Juvenile literature.

Classification: LCC SF395.4 C44 2019 | DDC 636.4009794—dc23

LC record available at https://lccn.loc.gov/2018039239

BOOK DESIGN BY KATIE KLIMOWICZ

Feiwel and Friends logo designed by Filomena Tuosto

First edition, 2019

The illustrations were created with graphite and digital painting.

1 3 5 7 9 10 8 6 4 2

mackids.com

For Beaudie.
Love, Dad

This is the true story behind who and what really saved Emma the pig.

The day Emma the pig arrived on the farm,
everyone was excited to meet her.

But Emma didn't have time to meet new friends,
because she was about to become a mama.
And there were two big problems . . .

Emma was skinny and sick.
I had to help her get healthy and plump
before the babies arrived.

I fed her all kinds of food.

Her favorite? **APPLES**!

Becoming a mama pig is a big job.
I hoped Emma would have a small litter—
no more than six piglets. We were
still working on getting her healthy

But before we could get Emma better, the big day arrived, and she started having babies!

FOUR,
FIVE,
SIX . . .

Just the right amount.

SEVEN, EIGHT.
NINE, TEN . . .

Tell me this will end!

Soon there were **SEVENTEEN** new hungry piglets for Emma to care for.

The next morning, Emma didn't look well. She had a fever.

Then poor Emma stopped
producing milk to feed her babies.

She was too sick. We had
to give Emma a break.

But who would take care of her seventeen piglets?

Until Emma got better, the piglets would live with us in our teeny-tiny farmhouse.

They splashed, burped, and slurped.

Seventeen piglets are messy!

Hopefully it would be a short stay.

The next day, Emma's fever was down. Hooray!
But she still wouldn't eat.

And if she wouldn't eat, she wouldn't be
strong enough to care for her babies.

We tried everything.

VEGGIES? Nope.

EGGS? Nope.

But then I remembered her most favorite food of all . . . **APPLES**!

Nope.

Nothing
worked.

The piglets stayed in our
tiny house. They whimpered,
sniffled, and snorted. They
missed their mama.

Then I got an idea of what might encourage
Emma to eat . . .

We brought the piglets back.

And it worked!
The piglets squiggled and
squealed, and Emma grunted
with glee.

She fed her babies.

Emma the pig finally started eating . . . **A LOT**!

Emma went right to work teaching the babies how to be pigs.

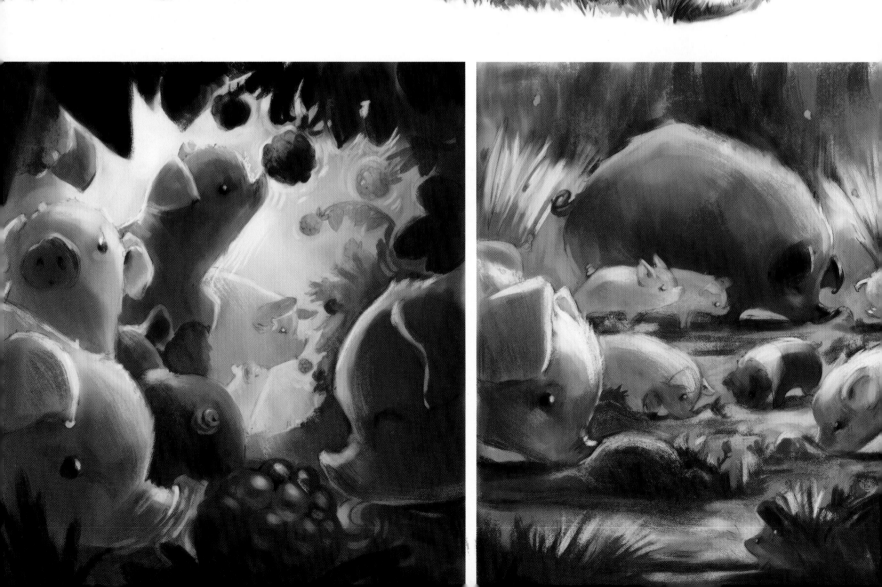

As the piglets grew,

they got to move into a pasture
of their own.

But Emma wasn't alone for long.

Soon she had a new friend: a scraggly little
rooster named Greasy—
red, just like her.

Today Emma is a much healthier sow.

She's even packed on a few pounds—200, to be exact.

We've all been inspired by the ways of Emma. Molly and I figured if she could raise seventeen . . .

we could raise one of our own.

I like to think Emma the pig was
saved by us.

But in the end it was her piggies who
gave her purpose.

As for Greasy and Emma . . .
they are still friends.

And that's a story for another day.

Molly and I started Apricot Lane Farms with a rather idealistic plan to turn an old depleted lemon farm into one that would grow hundreds of varieties of food all while working in complete harmony with nature. This was incredibly unrealistic, but we didn't know enough about farming to even doubt the possibilities. We would employ these old traditional farming methods to not only regenerate the soil and wildlife habitats but the entire ecosystem of our land. All of this would bolster a healthy and humane farming system to grow produce, raise livestock, and nourish us. But as I said, we were as green as the new grass in our pastures with no real farming experience. The first few years of our journey made it very clear—this was not going to be easy.

Over time we learned some tricks and it got better. This new life of ours revealed some deeper truths that we had not anticipated. Traditional farms of the past had no choice but to find creative ways to collaborate with nature in order to solve their farming challenges. And the way to this eco style of collaboration starts with a farmer's ability to see. And not just see, but see deeply into nature's inter-connected web of possibility. Nature has a language and a reason for everything. And the more we watched the more we saw. Suddenly our failures now contained answers—even pests had purpose—and our fears dissipated. This new way of seeing nature changed us. The lessons we were learning began having far greater implications beyond our tiny farm. Farming had given us a new perspective, a new lens with which to see not just our farm but ourselves and the world around us. I felt as if nature itself was reflecting back a deeper way to view our flawed human experience. These are the true stories about the animals and wildlife on our farm. Over the years, I have written them down and tucked them away in my nightstand. For me they have become an inspiring reminder of nature's capacity to lovingly embrace the imperfection of all life.

This picture of us was taken on December 12, 2018. The once red-haired Emma is a bit more gray—and more lovable, too, at seven hundred pounds. She's enjoying a lazy retirement in a pasture just outside my barn office window where she can easily call for her daily apple. Aside from that treat she gets a scoop of grain fermented in apple cider vinegar to maximize its digestion. She rounds out her diet by grazing the lush grass and uses her powerful nose to dig for grubs and roots as any healthy pig should.

A few folks to thank . . .

First, I must acknowledge my farming partner and beautiful wife, Molly Chester. She's my sparkly reminder that life itself is an opportunity and should never to be wasted in fear. To our passionate Apricot Lane Farms team, for whom I am so grateful. And to my publisher, Jean Feiwel, for presenting me with the opportunity to share these true stories. And my supportive editor, Liz Szabla, and the entire team at Feiwel & Friends—such a lovely and alive bunch. I'd also like to thank my producer, Sandra Keats; agent, Cathy Hemming; and of course the artist Jennifer L. Meyer, who captured the enchanting serenity of our farm. And lastly to my mom, Candy Chester, who knew long ago that the real Emma was no ordinary pig.

Maggie

The Orphan